LIZZIE AND THE TOOTH FAIRY

by Judith Wolman

illustrated by Karen Sukoneck

DANDELION BOOKS
Published by Dandelion Press, Inc.

For Emily

Ever since Lizzie was four years old, she had been looking forward to having a loose tooth. Now she was six, and most of her friends already had nice, big, empty spaces in their teeth. Jason was missing *both* of his bottom front teeth. He could stick out the tip of his tongue without opening his mouth.

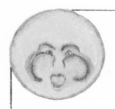

But Lizzie's teeth were all fastened firmly in her mouth, and, try as she might, she couldn't make them budge. Whenever she was watching television or reading a book, she would press her tongue against her bottom teeth, hoping to make them loosen up. Quite often she tried to wiggle them with her finger, but the only thing that moved was her finger.

One day Lizzie took a bite of an apple, and she felt something strange. She ran to the bathroom mirror to examine her mouth. When she pushed real hard, her tooth moved!

"At last, I have a loose tooth!" she cried. "Soon it will fall out and I'll have a lovely space. I'll put the tooth under my pillow and the Tooth Fairy will come. Maybe I'll wake up and see her, and talk to her. Maybe she'll even stay and play with me."

Lizzie was very excited, and every day she kept moving her tooth back and forth; it got looser and looser.

Lizzie's mother helped her make a special little pillow with a lace-edged pocket on the front for the tooth. The pillow was made of blue-and-white gingham, and was shaped like a heart. It had white lace all around the edge.

"If you put your baby tooth in this pocket when you go to sleep," said Lizzie's mother, "the Tooth Fairy will take it and leave a surprise in its place."

Lizzie couldn't wait for her tooth to fall out. Erika told her that her big brother once tied a string to his loose tooth, and then tied the other end of the string to a doorknob. He closed his eyes and asked Erika to slam the door. She did, and the tooth was yanked out of his mouth.

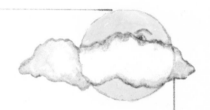

Lizzie had no intention of doing that! So she waited—but not very patiently. She wiggled her tooth with her tongue, and after a while she could even turn it around. It was barely attached, and Lizzie knew that it would come out any minute.

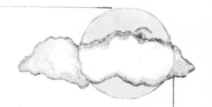

"Yay! My tooth! My tooth fell out! Mommy! Daddy! Look at my tooth! Hey, watch my tongue stick out through the hole! Where's my Tooth Fairy pillow? When can I go to bed?"

Lizzie couldn't wait to put her tooth under her pillow, and she went to sleep very early that night.

In the middle of the night Lizzie heard a sound. She opened her eyes and saw a beautiful little fairy perched on the edge of the bed. She was wearing a tiny blue gown, and a golden crown, and she carried a dainty wand with a shiny tooth on the end.

"Hi," said Lizzie. "You must be the Tooth Fairy."
"Indeed I am, Lizzie," replied the fairy.

Lizzie heard sweet music, and she got up and danced with the Tooth Fairy. They danced 'round and 'round, and sang, and laughed. Lizzie was having a wonderful time.

"Come with me, Lizzie," said the fairy. "You are my friend, and I want to show you where I live."

Lizzie followed the Tooth Fairy out through the garden, and over the clouds, until they came to a lovely castle.

The castle reached up to the stars, and inside there were lots and lots of teeth.

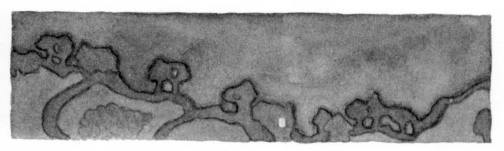

"Here are all the baby teeth I have collected from under children's pillows," said the fairy. "Look. These are Jason's front teeth, and here are two that belonged to Erika's brother Michael. This one here is rather old—it belonged to your Daddy until he was six, and I've had it ever since."

Lizzie could hardly believe her eyes. There were so many teeth she couldn't even count them. They were lined up in neat, long rows, and they were all so white and shiny!

"I take very good care of the teeth here," said the fairy. "I have a staff of little elves who brush the teeth every morning and every night. I hope you will take care of your new, grown-up teeth, Lizzie," she said. "You should brush them carefully after every meal, and go to the dentist regularly for check-ups. If you do, your teeth will stay shiny, and bright, and healthy, and you will be able to chew anything—even that terrible, tough meat that your mother sometimes gives you for dinner."

Lizzie looked around at the tremendous collection of baby teeth, and decided that she would be sure to brush her new tooth, and her old ones as well, as often as she could.

"Now we must get you back to bed," said the Tooth Fairy to Lizzie. "Your parents may come to tuck you in, and we wouldn't want them to find an empty bed."

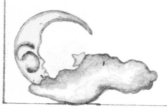

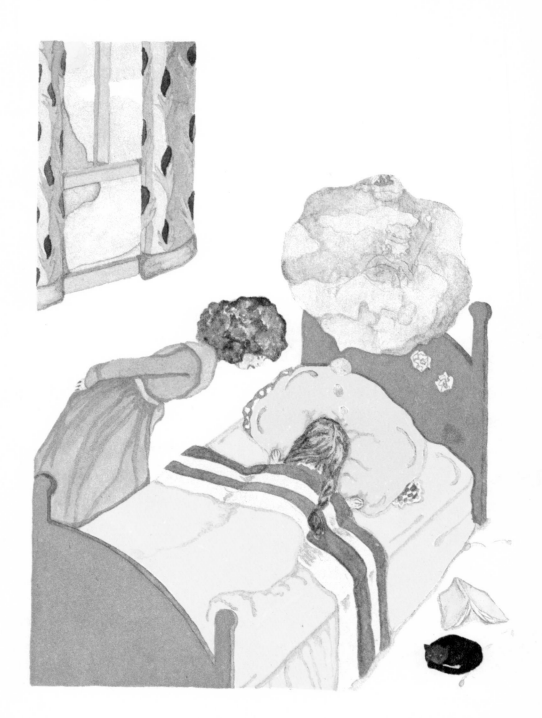

So they hurried down through the clouds, and into the garden, and as Lizzie nestled into her bed, the little fairy bent to kiss her good night.

But just then a familiar voice whispered, "Time to get up, Lizzie." Lizzie opened her eyes and saw her mother bending over to kiss her good morning.

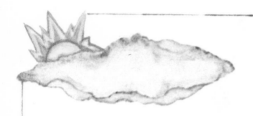

The first thing Lizzie did was to look inside her blue-and-white Tooth Fairy pillow. The little baby tooth was no longer in the pocket. In its place was a shiny, brand-new quarter.

"Oh, look what the Tooth Fairy left for me!" Lizzie exclaimed.

"How nice," said her mother. "I wonder what the Tooth Fairy does with all those baby teeth?"

"I wonder . . . " said Lizzie. And she smiled to herself.